This book belongs to

..Hannah Gibbons.

Tel 876146

The friends
Peter the Penguin
Pom the Panda

Benny the Cat   Teddy the Bear

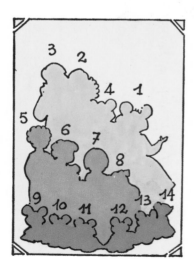

1. Mary Mouse
2. Mummy Doll
3. Daddy Doll
4. Whiskers Mouse
5. Pip
6. Melia
7. Roundy
8. Jumpy
9. Woffly
10. Scamper
11. Patter
12. Squeaker
13. Tiny
14. Frisky

Mary Mouse and the caravan

Enid Blyton

RAVETTE BOOKS

Contents

Chapter 1

Daddy Doll has an Accident

Who is this dear little mouse, peeping out of a doll's house window? Why, it's Mary Mouse, wearing her blouse covered with flowers and a crisp white apron over her black skirt! The Doll's House lies in the attic of a big house somewhere in France. It belongs to Daddy and Mummy Doll and the three doll children, Melia, Pip and Roundy. Mary Mouse looks after the house and the family. She sweeps and dusts

and washes and irons. She does all the shopping, and now she is about to make a cake in the little kitchen. Daddy Doll used to be a sailor. Mummy Doll is not very strong and has to rest a lot. Melia and Pip go to school.

But Roundy is the baby and stays at home with Mary Mouse. Mary's six children go to school too. The Mouse family live in a little home in the cellar. Mary's husband is Whiskers Mouse. He looks after the garden. The Doll family love Mary Mouse — and so do we!

One day when Mary Mouse was cleaning the Doll's House, Daddy Doll had a terrible accident. He went down the road to buy a paper, and stepped off the kerb just as a car was coming. Crash! The car bumped into Daddy Doll and knocked him right over. Poor Daddy Doll! The ambulance came and took him to hospital. And no one saw him go.

Soon a policeman came to tell Mummy Doll. He knocked on the door of the Doll's House. Mary Mouse let him in. Mummy Doll cried when the policeman told her. Mary Mouse comforted her.

"He will come
back in six
weeks' time," said
Mary Mouse.
"Now you drink
this cup of
tea and feel better!"
Then the police-
man told the three
children, Melia,
Pip and Roundy.
They went to
their mother, looking
very solemn. And
Jumpy went too.
"Mummy, we'll
be very good and
help you all
we can!" said Pip.
Mummy Doll
hugged them all.
"We shall look
after each other,"
she said.

Daddy Doll didn't earn any money while he was in hospital. And soon Mummy Doll had used up all the money he had saved. The money box was empty.

"You will have to leave us, Mary

13

Mouse," said Mummy Doll sadly. "I can't pay you or Whiskers any wages!"

"I shan't leave you," said Mary Mouse. "I'll go out to work three days a week and get some money." So off she went to Pom the Panda's house, and she cleaned all his cupboards out for him. Pom was very pleased and gave her five shillings, and Mary put it in Daddy Doll's money box at once. Then Whiskers Mouse went to see Benny the Cat. And Benny asked him to dig his garden for him. Whiskers dug thoroughly every day until it was finished. Benny gave him five shillings too.

Melia decided to earn some money. So she went to Mrs Busy and offered to take her baby out every day in the pram. Mrs Busy was pleased and gave her sixpence each time. Pip had a good idea. He borrowed Mary's shoe cleaning box, and went and sat at a muddy corner.

"Shine your shoes, sir?" he called. And Pom the Panda and Teddy the Bear stopped to have their shoes cleaned. Pip polished them well.

Little Roundy wanted to earn some money. So he took Mrs Busy's dog for a walk. But the dog was so big that it pulled poor Roundy along.

"It's taking me for a walk!" wailed poor Roundy. Melia hugged him when he put a penny in the money box.

"You are a great help!" she said.

Mary Mouse's children helped too. They made themselves into a little band, and they went to play on the street corner. Squeaker and Scamper played the trumpet, Frisky had a little drum and Patter and Tiny played the violin. Woffly did a little dance she had learned at school. And Jumpy went round with a hat belonging to Daddy Doll and collected quite a lot of pennies. Mummy Doll wasn't well enough to go to work, so she sold her pretty necklace for quite a lot of money. But it cost so much money to run a house with twelve people in it, not counting Jumpy, who ate as much as everybody else put together! And soon the money box was quite empty again.

Then one day there came a loud knock at the door. It was the landlord, Mr Fierce.

"I've come for the rent!" he said.

"Our money box is empty," said Mummy Doll. "Daddy Doll is in hospital. We can't pay you!"

Mr Fierce was angry. He shook his stick at poor Mummy Doll.

"I'll let someone else have the house!" he shouted, and he stamped off in a rage.

The very next day another family walked in at the front gate. It was Mr and Mrs Macdonald from the farm over the hill. Their farmhouse was being mended. Then all the farm animals came walking in at the gate. There were six cows, two pigs, three hens and a woolly sheep. But Jumpy flew at them barking madly. And would you believe it? They rushed off as fast as they could! And off went

Mr and Mrs Macdonald after them — and they didn't come back!

"Well, that's good," said Mary Mouse, and she made Mummy Doll and the children have a good tea to cheer them all up.

Then someone else came to see the house. It was Mr Jack-in-the-Box. He leapt out of his box as soon as Mary Mouse opened the door, and she squealed in fright. Whiskers heard her and came running up with a very big stick. Off went Mr Jack-in-the-Box, leaping along with his box, and they never saw him again!

Pip got very cross with people who wanted their house. So he got a big jug of water, and when he saw someone coming, he tipped up the jug — and soaked them! Mr Skittle got very wet and shouted loudly at

Pip, who ran downstairs in fright. Mary Mouse was very cross.

"It's no help to play tricks like that!" scolded Mary Mouse. "Now you just stand in the corner!" The little mice had watched Pip's trick.

"We'll do something now," they said. So they got a rope and tied it across the garden gate, so that somebody would fall over with a crash. And that night somebody did. *Crash*! *Bang*! *Thud*! Mary Mouse ran to the front door in a fright. Oh, dear! It was the policeman who was just coming round to see if everything was alright.

"You'll all go to bed without supper," said Mary Mouse to her six children. So they did.

Then Mr Fierce brought another family to the Doll's House. It was Daddy Rag Doll, Mummy Rag Doll and two very raggedy Doll children.

"Clear out by tomorrow, or I'll

bring the policeman!" shouted Mr
Fierce. Mummy Doll cried, and
Mary Mouse said:

"Oh dear! We shall have to go!"

Chapter 2

The Family Find a New Home

"But where shall we go to?" asked Mary Mouse. "Whiskers, you will have to find somewhere, and then we'll move."

Whiskers went off. Everyone began to pack. How sad they were! Mummy Doll packed six trunks and two boxes. Mary Mouse packed ten chests and three cases. Melia and Pip packed all their toys in a box.

"Oh, dear! When Daddy Doll comes out of hospital there'll be no home for him!" said Pip sadly.

Whiskers Mouse came back with a big barrow.

"We can all go and live with the Bunny Family," he said. "They live down a burrow not far off. They will put us up for a while." So the Doll's House family said goodbye to their little house, and went down the front path. Whiskers went to and fro with the barrow, collecting all their furniture and goods.

When Mary arrived at the burrow, she made friends with Mrs Flop Ears Bunny. They made beds for all the children in the burrow, and tucked them up firmly at bedtime. In the middle of the night Mary got up to see if the children were safe. Oh, dear! Melia, Pip and Roundy had gone! Where could they be? They had all felt cold, so each one of them had got into bed with a warm little bunny. They all looked so cosy that Mary couldn't bear to wake them!

The next day, Mummy Doll was so sad and ill that she couldn't get up. "I'll see to her," said Mrs Flop Ears.

So Mary took charge of all the children, and the young bunnies too. She dressed them up carefully and sent them off to school together. They streamed happily out of the rabbit hole, and played chase-me all the way to school.

That day Pom the Panda went to the Doll's House to call on the Doll family. He was very surprised to find the Rag Dolls there. He rushed off at once to find Benny the Cat, Teddy the Bear and Peter the Penguin.

"What can we do to help?" said Pom. "Let's empty our money boxes!"

So they did. And they took the money to Mr Fierce, the landlord.

"It's not nearly enough!" he said. Sadly, the four friends went off to the hospital to tell Daddy Doll what had happened.

"But I've got plenty of money!" said Daddy Doll jumping out of bed. "I hid it up the sitting-room chimney!"

He jumped out of bed and put his clothes on. "I'm almost better," he said. "I'll go and get the money now! But don't breathe a word to Mummy Doll, I want to surprise her." Daddy Doll went to ask Mr Fierce for permission to go to the old house but Mr Fierce refused, however Daddy Doll made up his mind to go that night to get his money anyway.

So he and Pom crept up to the Doll's House. It was empty! There was nobody there at all! The Rag Dolls had gone away! And when Daddy Doll and Pom climbed in at a window, they found a note on the table. It said:

We haven't any money to pay the rent. We are leaving

Daddy Doll and Pom went to the fireplace and felt up the chimney. The bag of money was still there! Daddy Doll and Pom danced for joy! The next morning they went to Mr Fierce, the landlord, and told him that the Rag Doll family had gone away.

"Without paying rent!" stormed Mr Fierce. "Oh, how I wish you had money, Daddy Doll! I'd have you back today!"

"But I have!" said Daddy Doll, and he emptied his bag at Mr Fierce's feet. "Enough rent for a year!" Then Pom the Panda and Daddy Doll made a little plan. They went to speak secretly to Mary Mouse. She was most surprised to see them.

"Take all the family to Pom's house for the night," said Daddy Doll. So Mary did. In the night she and Pom the Panda and Benny the Cat and Daddy Doll and Peter the Penguin and Whiskers Mouse and Teddy the Bear and Mr Flop Ears all moved the furniture back to the Doll's House. And Mary spent the rest of the night cleaning the house and everything in it. And Daddy Doll took a candle and went to pick flowers in the darkness for Mummy Doll's bedroom. And Whiskers mended everything the Rag Dolls had broken, with his hammer and

27

nails and glue. In the morning Mary Mouse baked a big cake and twenty-four buns and a lot of ginger biscuits. She fetched a sheet and sewed big red letters on it: WELCOME HOME! Pom and Teddy hung it up outside the front door. Then Mary and Whiskers Mouse went to fetch the family from Pom's house. Mummy Doll was still in bed.

"I feel so ill!" she told Mary. "I want Daddy Doll! I want my own little house again!"

"Get up!" said Mary. "I've found the loveliest house you ever saw. And it's all ready for you!"

Then everyone left Pom's house and went with Mary Mouse. And she took them right home to their own Doll's House. And there was Daddy Doll standing under the WELCOME HOME! Mummy Doll fell into his arms and cried for joy!

Then what a tea party there was!

Even Jumpy had a chair, and he ate
thirteen sandwiches and a half! Mary
Mouse cut the enormous cake.
There was a slice for everyone, not
forgetting the six mouse children.

Mummy Doll stood up with a
glass of lemonade in her hand.

"Here's to our house and to Mary
Mouse!" she cried.

Then Melia, Pip and Roundy gave
Mary Mouse big hugs. "We do love
you, Mary Mouse!"
they cried. "We do! We do!"

Chapter 3

Mary Mouse Goes Out for the Day

One day Mummy and Daddy Doll decided to go off for a holiday together. They hired a little car. They were very excited as they got in, all ready to go. Pip carried Mummy Doll's bag and put it in the car. Melia picked a big red rose for Mummy Doll to wear.

"A red rose means 'I love you,' Mummy!" said Melia. Roundy wanted to do something too. So he gave Mummy Doll his best ball.

"You can play with it!" he said. Then Daddy started up the car, hooted the horn, and away they went.

"Be good, children!" cried Mummy Doll. Mary Mouse shooed the three children indoors. They looked very sad.

"Cheer up!" said Mary Mouse. "Look I've made you cherry buns! You can each have one now — two if you like!"

Melia, Pip and Roundy missed Mummy and Daddy Doll very much. Melia and Roundy cried. So Mary Mouse found them jobs to do.

"Melia, go and fetch the mouse children from school for me!" she said.

"Roundy, go and pick

strawberries for dinner — you can
eat three yourself!"

So Melia fetched the little mice.
They were very pleased to see her.
And Roundy went to pick
strawberries — but he ate more than
he put in the basket. And very soon

he had such a pain in his tummy that
he sat down and cried again!

"You give him a ride on your
bicycle, Pip!" said Mary. "Dear me!
I'm wishing already that Mummy
Doll was back again!"

The children soon settled down
again. And a few days later, the little

mouse children came running home in delight.

"Mummy Mouse, where are you? We've been asked to go for a day by the sea! Farmer Straw says he'll lend you his donkey cart!"

"How nice of him!" said Mary Mouse. "But I can't leave Melia, Pip and Roundy by themselves. So you can't go!"

The mouse children cried loudly in disappointment, so Melia, Pip and Roundy begged Mary Mouse to take them for their day's outing.

"Do . . . do go!" said Melia. "We can manage everything for ourselves.

Mummy Doll would want you to go!"

Pip nodded his head:

"Melia can do the shopping that day. I can clean the rooms. And Roundy can help with the dusting!"

"Well, Whiskers Mouse will keep his eye on you," said Mary Mouse. "But do . . . do be good now!"

So, when the day came and Farmer Straw drove up in his donkey cart, Mary Mouse was ready. All the six mouse children were ready too, with their spades and buckets. How excited they were! They drove off with Mary Mouse, waving their spades in the air. Woffly even knocked off Mary Mouse's hat!

"Now see that you're good!" said

Whiskers Mouse to Melia, Pip and
Roundy. "I'll be busy in the
garden."

"Let's be very, VERY good and

helpful," said Melia, excited to be all on their own. "What shall we do?"

"Well, you go and do the shopping, of course," said Pip. "And mind you buy some nice things!"

So Melia went out carrying Mary Mouse's enormous shopping basket. She went first to the grocer's and bought a big pineapple, because they all liked pineapple so much.

"Please put it on the week's bill," she said.

Then she went to the baker's and looked in his window. "We'll be very hungry by teatime," she thought. So she asked for a nice big chocolate cake, a jam sponge, some sugar biscuits and six little tarts. And she put those on the bill too. Then she went to the butcher's. She bought twelve sausages.

"Jumpy likes them too!" she said. "Please put them on the bill!"

Melia went to the sweet shop!

"Three bars of chocolate, please!"
she said. "And a box of sweets, and
five lollipops!"

Melia's basket was now quite full
and dreadfully heavy. She stopped
to put it down and a big black cat
pounced on the sausages. Melia had
to smack the cat and go home
fast!

Pip and Roundy were very busy
too. As soon as Melia had gone out,
the fire began to smoke.

"Look at that now!" said Pip,
coughing. "The chimney wants
sweeping. Go and tell the sweep to
come, Roundy!"

So Roundy trotted off to the
sweep's house and knocked at the
door.

"Please, our chimney's smoking!"
said Roundy. "Can the sweep
come?"

"No, he can't," said Mrs Sweep.
"He's gone to a wedding today, and

nice and clean he looks too, for a
change!"

Roundy saw the sweep's poles and
brush standing in a shed nearby.

"Can we borrow those?" he asked.

"Well, you ask Mr Whiskers if he
can sweep the chimney for you,"
said Mrs Sweep. "He'll know how
to."

So off went little Roundy, dragging
the poles and brush behind him.
"Sweep, Sweeeeep!" he called,

proudly. He told Pip that Mr Sweep couldn't come.

"We must ask Whiskers instead," he said.

"Whiskers has gone to fetch his wheelbarrow from the carpenter," said Pip. "It had to be mended."

"Well — let's sweep the chimney ourselves then," said Roundy excited. "It's quite easy . . . "

"We'd better not," said Pip.

But Roundy began to fit the poles together. Pip felt excited too.

"It would be fun to sweep the chimney!" he said. "I've let the fire out. We could do it now!"

So they fitted the brush on a pole and then fitted all the poles together.

"Up the chimney goes the brush!" said Pip, and he pushed it up with Roundy helping.

The poles went up and up. Roundy went outside to look. Yes! The brush had come out of the top,

frightening a big rook! But as the
brush went up, something else came
down! Soot — black, dirty soot —
came down and flew all over the
room, and flew all over Pip and
Roundy too. When Melia came in
with the shopping, she screamed
with fright.

"Who are you? Where have you
come from? Go away!"

"It's us, Pip and Roundy!" said
Pip. "We're sweeping the chimney
because the
fire smoked!"

"You bad
naughty boys!"
said Melia,
beginning to cry.
"See how
dirty the room
is! I'll have
to scrub it all
over. Go upstairs
and wash yourselves

clean! But take the poles and the brush outside first. You BAD boys!"

Melia was very cross indeed. She went to fetch a pail of water and a brush and a cloth to clean the room. Pip and Roundy went upstairs. They left a trail of black footsteps all the way up. They filled the bath and scrubbed each other until they were clean. When they came down, poor Melia was still scrubbing the room.

"We're hungry!" said Pip. "What have you brought for dinner, Melia? Can we have it in the garden?"

"Yes," said Melia. "This room smells of soot. I bought some sausages. I'll get them out and cook them!" But when Melia got to the kitchen, the sausages had gone.

"Oh, dear!" said Melia. "I forgot to put them away! Someone has taken them. It must be that bad Jumpy!

And there was Jumpy, running

down the garden, dragging the sausages behind him!

"There goes our dinner!" wept Melia. "We'll just have to have chocolate cake and jam tarts and pineapple" But the next door dog had gone off with the chocolate cake and the jam sponge! There was only the pineapple, the tarts and the biscuits for dinner.

"I do want sausages!" wailed Roundy.

At that moment they heard a strange noise.

"It's like running water!" said Pip. And that is what it was! Pip had left the bath taps running and the bath had overflowed — and the water was running down the stairs like a waterfall. Melia ran upstairs to turn the taps off. Pip opened the front door to let out the water.

Whiskers Mouse was just bringing back the mended barrow. He was most surprised to see the water.

"Now what have you three been doing?" he asked. Whiskers mopped up all the water. He lit the fire to dry everything. And he boiled eggs for their dinner.

"You have been bad and silly," he said. "Mary Mouse will be cross!"

At that moment Mary Mouse walked in. She *was* cross.

"You must pay for the sausages and the cake from your own money, Melia," she said. "And you'll chop firewood for me all tomorrow, Pip."

"And you'll help Whiskers with the weeding, Roundy!"

So Melia paid for the sausages and the cake and helped Mary with the washing. Pip chopped wood and Roundy weeded. How tired they were at the end of the day! Then Mary Mouse forgave them, and read

them their favourite good night
story.

Chapter 4

A Caravan Holiday

When Daddy and Mummy Doll came back everyone was very happy. For a while there were no more adventures.

Then one day Daddy Doll came home and called them all together.

"I have borrowed two caravans and we will go off and have a holiday."

What a surprise for everyone! The very next day the caravans arrived, pulled by two friendly horses. One horse was small and black with a white star. He was called Beauty. The other was big with shaggy

hooves and a thick mane and tail. He was brown, so they called him Brownie.

Mummy Doll started to pack. The Mouse family packed too and soon they were ready to go. Mummy Doll,

Melia, Pip and Roundy climbed into
the first caravan and Daddy got up
behind Brownie. Mary and her six
children got into the other caravan
and Whiskers drove Beauty. And off
they went down the road, leaving
the little Doll's House behind, with
Jumpy the dog to guard it.

That night the caravans stopped
beside a stream in a field. All the

children got out.

"Pip! You take the mouse
children, and go and get firewood for
a fire," called Daddy Doll.

Soon Pip and the mice came back
with armfuls of twigs. What a fire

they built! When it was blazing, Mummy Doll and Mary Mouse cooked a fine dinner on it.

"It does smell good!" said Pip. They all sat down in a ring round the fire and ate their dinner. It tasted very good!

"Now Melia! You and three of the mouse children must wash up!" said Mummy Doll. "Mary and I want a rest."

Melia was very good and began to wash up. But Woffly, Patter and Tiny were naughty and ran off to play hide-and-seek. When Mary and Whiskers Mouse found them, they sent them off to bed. Melia saw them looking sadly out of the window.

Soon it was time for the children to go to bed in the bunks in their caravan. Melia had the one under the window as she wanted to see outside. When the stars came out, everyone was asleep. Suddenly

Melia woke up in fright! Something was looking in at the caravan window near her head!

"Help! Help!" squealed Melia. "It's a burglar!"

Daddy Doll jumped out of his bunk. He switched on his torch. How he laughed!

"Why, it's only a cow looking in at the window, Melia!"

So it was! Melia felt rather silly! The cow trotted off to tell its friends about Melia. It was laughing too!

Next morning Whiskers Mouse sent three mouse children to the stream to get water. But Frisky, Scamper and Squeaker were silly, and pushed each other into the water. And they were sent to bed, like the girl mice. They were cross!

"We'd better be good," said Pip to Melia and Roundy. "Everybody's being sent to bed!"

They all went off in the caravans

again that day. In the afternoon they saw something very exciting!

"It's a fair! It's a fair!" shouted Pip. "Look! There's a roundabout!"

Sure enough, there was a fair. The roundabout was very big. It had all kinds of animals to ride on. Mummy Doll gave the children a penny each for a ride.

"Thank you!" they said.

Melia chose a swan. She held onto its neck and felt very proud. Pip chose an elephant. How high up he was! Roundy chose a duck. He thought that would be nice and safe. What do you think the six mouse children chose? A great big cat! "Look! Look! We're riding a cat!" they cried.

Melia and Roundy went in a swing boat together. Pip went to knock some coconuts off sticks. But he threw so badly that he hit the coconut man. The man was angry

and ran after Pip, shouting loudly.
Pip was afraid and ran to his
caravan. He climbed quickly up to
the roof and lay flat. The coconut
man couldn't see him anywhere. He
shook his fist and went back to his
coconuts. Pip didn't dare to come
down. Eventually he fell asleep.
Mummy Doll missed him and called
him. But no Pip came! Suddenly
Mary Mouse saw a foot hanging
over the caravan top. And there she
found Pip fast asleep. She lifted him
down and scolded him.

"You bad boy! Lying on the dirty
roof! You just get into your bunk
and I'll wash your trousers!"

So poor Pip missed the rest of the
fair. But the six mice children
brought him the coconut he had
won. So he happily ate a big slice
while they nibbled bits, too.

Melia was happy because she had
thrown a ring over an alarm clock,

and won it. She gave it to Mary
Mouse who was very pleased.

"You're a good child," she said.
"Thank you!"

The next day they went on again,
and came to a little farm.

"Let's stay here for a few days!"
said Mummy Doll.

So they did. Melia learned to milk
a cow. Pip went to pick flowers in a
field with Roundy. But when they
went away, they left the gate open.

And all the farmer's sheep ran out of the field into the road! The farmer was cross! He chased the sheep back with a stick and then — oh, dear! He chased Pip and Roundy with a stick too!

They ran as fast as their legs would carry them.

"Horrid man!" wept Roundy. "I won't go near him again. He did frighten me!" And he howled loudly.

The next day when Melia, Pip and Roundy were out with Mary Mouse for a walk, Melia found eight hen's eggs under a hedge.

"Look!" she said. "A hen has laid away from home!"

"We'll take them back," said Pip, and he began to pick them up.

"Yes! We won't give them back to that horrid horrid farmer!" said Roundy looking fierce. But Mary Mouse was shocked.

"Of course we must take them

back to the farm!" she said. "They don't belong to us!" And she made Melia, Pip and Roundy go to the farm door. The farmer opened the door.

"P-p-p-please, we've f-f-found some eggs under the hedge!" said Melia. "So we've brought them to you!"

"What nice children!" said the farmer smiling. "Come along in! My wife is baking chocolate buns."

And, dear me! Soon the three children were sitting in the kitchen and the farmer took Roundy on his knee to eat a chocolate bun. What a surprise!

"It's nice to see honest children," said the farmer's wife. "Do have some ginger biscuits too!"

"There," said Melia, when they

walked back to the caravan. "It's good that you did the right thing, isn't it?"

They had a lovely time at the farm. Pip rode the biggest horse. Melia rode a grey pony and Roundy rode a very fat, little pony. And the six little mouse children all got onto the back of Billy the Goat and sat in a row. Suddenly the goat tossed them all up in the air and over the hedge. And they came down in the tub of hot water that Mary Mouse had borrowed from the farmer's wife to do her washing!

So what do you think she did? She took Frisky and Scamper and Squeaker and Woffly and Patter and Tiny, and pegged them all out on the line to dry. There they hung in the wind and couldn't get down, until Mary unpegged them!

"Now you're dry!" she said. "Off you go!"

After a few days they set off again. Brownie went first, pulling the Doll family's caravan, and Beauty followed. They came to a very steep hill. Up went Brownie, panting and puffing, with his caravan. And behind him came Beauty. But something went wrong. Melia gave a scream as she saw Mary Mouse's caravan running backwards, leaving poor Beauty standing alone, looking puzzled. The caravan went faster and faster down the hill in a cloud of dust! Melia screamed again!

Then Mummy and Daddy Doll and Pip and Roundy saw what was happening.

"It will be smashed to bits!" wept Mummy Doll. "Poor Mary Mouse and Whiskers and the children!"

Trembling and frightened, they all went down the hill looking for the lost caravan. It was nowhere to be seen. Where could it be? But what was that in the pond? Yes, it was the caravan — upside down — floating in the pond with its wheels in the air! Out of the window climbed Mary Mouse with three of the six mouse children. And after her came Whiskers with the other three. They waded out of the pond, surrounded by surprised ducks.

"Are you hurt?" cried Mummy Doll.

But except that Mary had to have her head bound up and Squeaker had to have his leg bandaged, no one was hurt.

"I want to go home," wailed Squeaker. "I don't like caravans any more!"

"We'll all go home," said Daddy Doll. "First we will get the caravan out, and dry it — then back we'll go!"

Mummy Doll wrote to Peter the Penguin and Pom the Panda and asked them to open up the house for them. Peter and Pom told Teddy the Bear and Benny the Cat and they all went round to the Doll's House. Jumpy the dog, who had been guarding the house for the family, was so pleased to see them!

"I've been so very lonely!" he barked. Teddy and Pom put on aprons and swept and dusted. Peter the Penguin went out shopping with Benny the Cat. Then they put vases of flowers everywhere and wound up the clocks. They made all the beds and put hot water bottles in them.

Then the two caravans drew up at the gate. What an excitement! Jumpy nearly went mad! He ran round and round and barked. Into the house went Mummy and Daddy  Doll, Melia, Pip and Roundy and Mary Mouse and Whiskers and the six mice children. "Oh, it's so good to be home again!" said Mummy Doll, and all the children cheered. And Jumpy wagged his tail so hard that it almost fell off. What a happy day!

Chapter 5

The Garden Party

One day, when Mary Mouse was out shopping with Melia, Pip and Roundy, she saw a little girl doll crying. Mary Mouse comforted her. "What's the matter?" she asked.

"I'm lost!" the little girl sobbed! "Somebody lost me!"

"Now, don't cry!" said kind Mary Mouse. "We will take you to the Home for Lost Toys. Come along!"

Away they all went down the road. And there was the Home for Lost Toys with a bright red roof and a bright red door! A kind nurse came out to see them.

"Oh — *another* lost toy!" she said. "Come in, my dear!"

Mary, Melia, Pip and Roundy all went into the Home — and dear me! What a lot of toys there were!

"I was lost last week!" said a cuddly teddy bear.

"And I was lost a whole year ago!" said a smiling monkey.

"Can you take this lost doll?" asked Mary Mouse. "I'd take her home myself, but our Doll's House is full."

"Yes, of course I'll have her," said the kind nurse doll, and she took the lost doll on her knee. "But, oh dear! It does cost such a lot to keep lost toys here! If we only had more money! See! Our money box is empty!"

Mary Mouse went back to the little Doll's House with Melia, Pip and Roundy. They were all thinking hard. Mary Mouse went straight to Mummy Doll and told her about the Home for Lost Toys.

"We must do something to help," she said.

"Of course!" said Mummy Doll. "And Melia, Pip and Roundy must help too!"

So Mary Mouse took a big sheet of paper and wrote down what everyone should do.

"We will have a garden party," she said, writing fast. "Melia, get your knitting wool at once! You must knit some things to sell!" So Melia fetched her wool.

"Pip, you must get your carpentry set, and make all kinds of things."

So Pip brought his set of tools — and even Roundy wanted to help!

"We'll buy balloons to sell, and you shall blow them up for me," said Mary Mouse.

"I'll sew some baby clothes," said Mummy Doll, and fetched her work basket.

"And I'll borrow two little donkeys from the farm, and let children have rides on them," said Daddy Doll.

Then how busy everyone was! Mary Mouse was the busiest of all. She began making jam to sell at the garden party. And all her children were sent to pick blackberries for her jam — so they worked hard as well! Whiskers Mouse said he would grow flowers to sell at the garden party, and he was busy too.

Daddy Doll went to the farm to ask about the donkeys.

"Yes, certainly you shall have them!" said the farmer. "I will make sure they know how to behave themselves."

Melia knitted and knitted. She made three jerseys, three pairs of

socks and a warm jacket. Pip made
a little stool and a bookshelf and
some wooden toys.

"I didn't know you were so
clever!" said Mummy Doll. The
mouse children brought in so many
baskets of blackberries that Mary
Mouse made fifty pots of jam! And
she bottled some plums that
Whiskers brought in too.

Then Pip and Melia made notices
about the garden party.

> Everyone come to our
> **Garden Party**
> next Sunday at 2 o'clock
> in aid of
> the home for lost toys ✳

The mouse children rushed off to put them through letterboxes.

At last the great day came. Melia looked out of the window.

"It's a fine day!" she cried. "Look, Pip and Roundy! The sun is shining in the sky!"

Mary Mouse had told everyone what to do.

Daddy Doll and Whiskers put up the stalls and draped them with clean cloths. Mary Mouse and Mummy Doll cut sandwiches and made cakes for sale at tea time. Roundy blew up the balloons. Oh, Roundy! Be careful! You are blowing up that one too much! There! It's burst with a bang! Roundy fell over backwards, but he didn't mind.

Pip arranged all the things he had made on his stall. Melia had a stall, too, for all the clothes she had knitted. Next door was Mummy Doll's stall with such a lot of beautiful baby clothes! Mary Mouse had a stall for her jam and the bottles of plums, and Whiskers had one for his flowers. Soon it was 2 o'clock. The farmer and his wife arrived first with their donkeys. Daddy gave each one a carrot and led them off down the garden. Next came Pom the

Panda and Peter the Penguin.

"Come along and buy!" cried Pip.

"I'd like to buy this nice little stool," said Pom, and he paid Pip a shilling for it. Pip was *so* pleased!

"I'll have three jars of blackberry jam and a bottle of plums," said Peter to Mary Mouse. Then came Teddy the Bear and Benny the Cat.

"I want some woolly socks," said Benny. Melia sold him two pairs.

Soon the garden was full of people. There was Mrs Curly Hair Doll with her five children and Mr Postman and his wife. Mrs Postman bought some clothes from Mummy Doll's stall. Mary Mouse's friend Mary Mary Quite Contrary came too.

"I'll have some jam," she said.

Daddy Doll was busy all afternoon. All Mrs Curly Hair Doll's children had rides, and when Mrs Skittle came with her six children there was quite a long queue.

At tea time Mummy Doll and Mary Mouse were very busy. They sold lots of sandwiches and cakes. Melia and Pip carried round cups of tea and glasses of lemonade, and took a penny for each one.

"Mummy, I've sold everything on my stall!" said Pip. "Can I have a donkey ride now?"

"And I've sold everything too!" said Melia. "Just feel my bag of

money!"

At last everyone went home.

"Thank you for a lovely garden party," they said when they left.

"We do like the things we have bought!"

"Now we will count up our money," said Daddy Doll.

Everybody emptied their money onto the grass. What a pile there was! Daddy put it all into Whiskers Mouse's wheelbarrow, and they took it straight to the Home for Lost Toys. The nurse doll cried tears of joy when she saw it.

"I'll buy a new pram — and some cots!" she said. "You are kind!"

"You're to buy the lost toys some sweets with my balloon money!" said Roundy.

"Come along!" said Mary Mouse. "We must go back home and clear up everything in the garden."

So back they went. When

everything was tidied away, Mary Mouse gave the children their supper and read them their favourite story.

"I'm tired," said Melia. "But I'm very, very happy. Isn't it a lovely feeling to work hard and be kind, Mary Mouse?"

Yes, Melia it is! Now you must all sleep well.

Chapter 6

The Naughty Donkey

One morning Mary Mouse got up early as usual, and heard someone knocking at the door. Knock! Knock! Knock! She ran to open it. Standing outside was a little grey donkey!

"Dear me!" said Mary Mouse.

"How pleased Melia, Pip and Roundy will be to see you!" And she called loudly,

"Melia! Pip! Roundy! Someone to see you!"

The children ran downstairs.

"Oh, what a dear little donkey!" said Pip.

"Whose is he?" asked Melia and stroked the big soft nose.

"I don't know," said Mary Mouse. "Let's take him into the back garden."

It wasn't long before the donkey was nibbling grass there, swishing his tail. And it wasn't long before Melia, Pip and Roundy were on his back. But the donkey ran away with them down the street! Mary Mouse was very upset.

"They will fall off!" she said. "Where's my bicycle? I must go after them and make sure they're all right!"

Mary Mouse told everyone she met how a runaway donkey had gone off with Melia, Pip and Roundy. They all fetched their bicycles and pedalled down the road as fast as they could.

They passed the Noah's Ark, and Mr Noah came out in surprise.

"Where are you all going?" he asked. When they told him, he caught one of his horses and joined in the chase. The donkey did lead them a dance! He splashed through a big pond. He

even crossed some railway lines, and it was very dangerous because there was a train coming!

"Oh stop, donkey! Stop!" begged Melia. "I'm almost falling off your back!"

But the donkey was enjoying himself too much to stop. It jumped over a gate into the road and galloped into a handcart of potatoes. How angry the potato man was! Melia began to fall. *Bump*! The donkey went on without her.

"I'm going to find a policeman," said Mary Mouse. "That's a very bad donkey. Come along everyone!"

A little rabbit took Melia to the police station too.

They all told the policeman what had happened.

"Ha! That donkey belongs to the circus," said the policeman. "His name is Stamper!"

"Well, he can certainly stamp!"

said Melia. "But do please go after him! Pip and Roundy are on his back."

"I'll get my bicycle," said the big policeman. "Hop on the back, will you?"

So Melia went off on the back of the policeman's bicycle. How everyone stared!

Meanwhile, Stamper was still galloping away. He came to a big stream, and pulling his body together he gave a great JUMP! But splash! He landed in the water. Pip and Roundy fell off on the bank.

"Oh, you've made me so wet!" cried Pip. "Stop, donkey! Stop! We've fallen off!" The policeman rode up with Melia.

"Never mind," he said kindly. "I'll soon dry you with my big hanky."

The donkey was tired. It had run so far and so fast.

"Look, we can catch it easily now!" said the policeman. "Don't frighten it!" So very quietly indeed they walked over to the panting donkey.

"Ha! Caught you, you bad little thing!" said the policeman.

Just then there came the sound of music. And Melia saw a roundabout and a big circus tent nearby in a field. And then they heard bicycle bells, and all the others rode up over

the bumpy field on their bicycles,
with Mary Mouse in the lead.

"Oh, you bad donkey!" said Pip.
"What did you mean by tearing
away with us?" The circus
man came running up.
"I'm sorry my
donkey was naughty!"
he said. "Would
you like a ride
on the roundabout
to make up for it?"

"Oh, yes please!" said Melia.
"But I'm afraid we haven't any
money!"

"I shan't charge you anything,"
said the circus man kindly. "I'm just
pleased to have my donkey back."
So the children and Mary Mouse
and all their friends climbed onto the
roundabout. Pip rode on a horse.
Roundy got on a big elephant. Mary
Mouse rode on a lion. And Melia
climbed onto a giraffe.

When they had finished their ride, the circus man said to Mary Mouse, "You must all come and see my circus on Saturday!"

"Yes, we will!" said the children.

"What an exciting day we've had!" said Melia as they went home. "I've loved every minute!"

Chapter 7

The Circus

The children were very excited. Today was the day of the circus!

"You must be very good before we go," said Mary Mouse. "Melia, you must wash up! Pip you must clean the shoes!"

Melia and Pip were very good. Roundy helped with the shoes, but most of the polish went on himself. Jumpy went to fetch Daddy Doll's

newspaper. That evening they all
set off together. They arrived at
the circus in the dark. Inside there
were bright lights. It was very
exciting! They found their seats
and waited for the circus to begin.
Jumpy sat on Mummy Doll's knee
so that he could see better. The
clowns came on first.

"Look at the one with the great
big red nose!" squealed Roundy.
"I want a nose like that!"

"Oh, there's one with enormously long legs!" said Melia. "He must be on stilts. Isn't he tall!"

The clowns turned head over heels, and smacked each other with balloons that went pop! Then in came the horses! The ring master cracked his whip, and they galloped this way

and that so gracefully. Suddenly a
man ran in, wearing a glittering coat
and trousers. He bowed to everyone.
Then he began to climb a ladder that
went right up into the roof of the
circus tent. At last he reached a rope
that stretched right over the circus
ring. And then he began to run!
When he reached the other end, he
turned and back he went again.
Everyone cheered when he slid
quickly down the ladder.

After that six little poodles ran into
the ring and began to perform.

"Look, Jumpy!" said Daddy Doll.
"They are even cleverer than you!"

Jumpy was so excited that he leapt
off Mummy Doll's knee and rushed
into the ring barking! He began to
play ball with the poodles. He even
walked on his hind legs when they
did! He was really very clever! But
Daddy Doll called him back and
made him sit down again.

Then the clowns came back. Two
of them had pails of water. They
threw them all over the others! One

of the wet clowns fetched a garden hose — and watered the two naughty clowns. Then he watered the ring master who was very angry, and cracked his whip.

All the clowns ran off, howling. The ring master cracked his whip again. And in came a great white bear riding on a bicycle. He rode it round the ring and even rang the bell. Then he got in a little car and drove that round the ring. When he had finished he got out and bowed. Everyone cheered and clapped! Suddenly the bear put up his paws and took off his great bear head. He wasn't a real bear at all, but a smiling young man dressed up as a bear!

Then into the ring came a little donkey. He had pompoms on his harness, which swayed as he trotted in. Then he stood still and stamped his foot in time to the music.

"It's Stamper!" It's Stamper!"
cried Pip. "Isn't he clever!" Stamper
trotted round the ring, and played
with the clowns before he went out.

At last it was time for the final
parade. Everyone cheered and
Jumpy barked loudly.

"Oh, I did love it all!" said Melia.
"Let's see it again tomorrow!"

But Mummy Doll said, "No!"

"We'll make a circus of our own!"
said Melia. So they put up a rope

round a ring of grass. And Pip made himself into a funny clown with a red nose. And Melia brought out the rocking horse and pretended to ride it standing up. Roundy got Pip's drum, and his own toy trumpet for the band. And Jumpy was a performing dog. The little mouse children sat on the grass and watched. At the end they clapped hard. Mummy and Daddy Doll clapped too. And Mary Mouse brought everyone an ice cream to eat.

"Thank you! Thank you, Mary Mouse!"